To Bed, To Bed!

by MISCHA RICHTER

Prentice-Hall, Inc.
Englewood Cliffs, New Jersey

Copyright © 1981 by Mischa Richter
All rights reserved. No part of this book may be
reproduced in any form, or by any means, except
for the inclusion of brief quotations in a review,
without permission in writing from the publisher.
Printed in the United States of America   ·J
Prentice-Hall International, Inc., London
Prentice-Hall of Australia, Pty. Ltd., North Sydney
Prentice-Hall of Canada, Ltd., Toronto
Prentice-Hall of India Private Ltd., New Delhi
Prentice-Hall of Japan, Inc., Tokyo
Prentice-Hall of Southeast Asia Pte. Ltd. Singapore
Whitehall Books Limited, Wellington, New Zealand

10 9 8 7 6 5 4 3 2 1

Library of Congress Cataloging in Publication Data
Richter, Mischa.   To bed, to bed.
Summary: Unwilling to go to bed because it is
still light outside, a young prince takes a long,
adventurous route through the castle to his bedroom.
[1. Bedtime–Fiction. 2. Princes–Fiction]
I. Title.   PZ7.R4155To   1981   [E]
81-2250   ISBN 0-13-922922-1   AACR2

To my three grandsons,
Sacha, Mischa and Will.

One day, as the royal family was taking a walk in the palace garden, the king turned to his son and said, "It is time for bed."

"But, Father, the sun is still shining," answered the prince.

"Do as you are told," said the queen.

So the prince went off to bed.

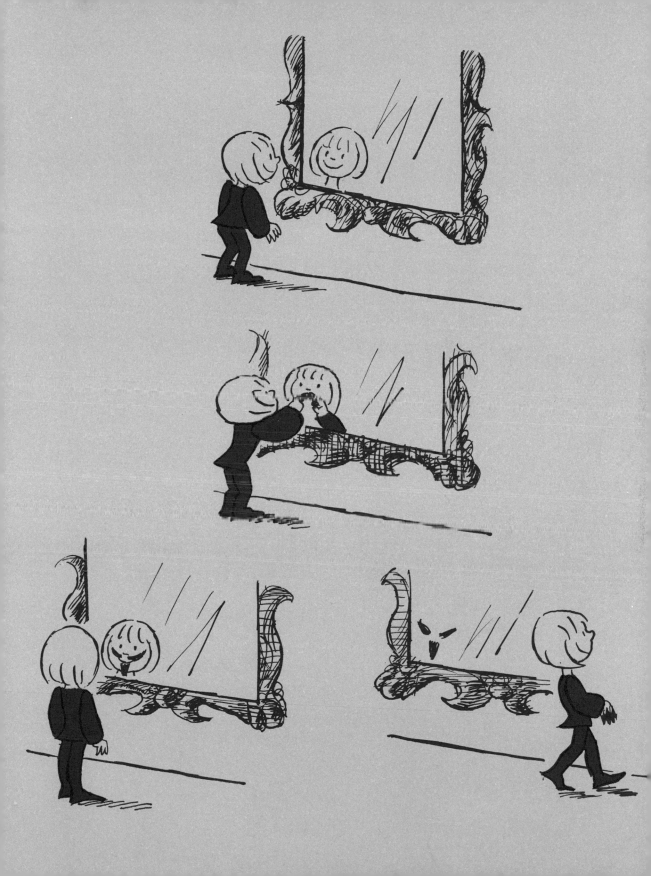

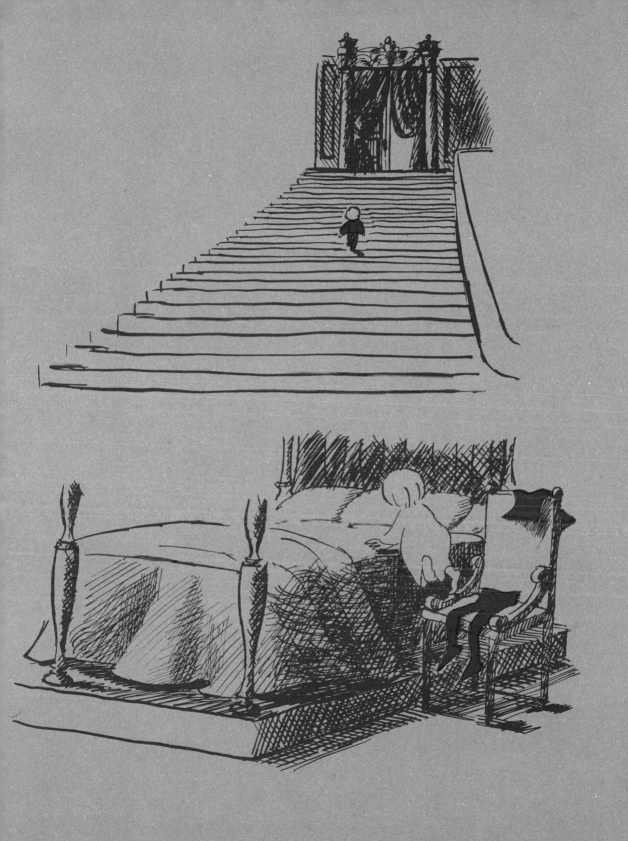